Confessions
(Scenes, Inner Thoughts, Histories)

also by I Kyūu

Lord Su (Ten Tales of Who He Was)
Lightning the Load
More Tales of Lord Su

Confessions
(Scenes, Inner Thoughts, Histories)

by
I Kyūu

Poetic Justice Books & Arts
Port Saint Lucie, Florida

book design and layout: SpiNDec, Port Saint Lucie, FL
cover image: *Vine,* 2017, Kris Haggblom

Published by Poetic Justice Books
Port Saint Lucie, Florida
www.poeticjusticebooks.com

ISBN: 978-1-950433-05-6

FIRST EDITION
10 9 8 7 6 5 4 3 2 1

Confessions have different forms. They
may be spoken or silent. They may reveal
what was hidden or ask for forgiveness.
They may do neither of those.

Confessions
(Scenes, Inner Thoughts, Histories)

Our confessions, spoken or silent,
reveal what is hidden. They may have
another quality.

THE WALLS OF MY CELL ARE scarred with
the etchings of its former inhabitant. Each morning,
I dip my hands in a fresh bowl of water. I raise them
to my face. I let the air dry hands and face. Then I
am ready. I trace some etchings with my fingertips.
When I complete tracing all the etchings, I start again.
This has become my way to pay homage to one who
drew them. It is also a way to recognize the beauty
we hold in us.

The weight of your secret is now my friend. I have
no other way to describe it. In keeping your secret, I hold
it as I would the words of a loved one. The words that
pass between us are not spoken. They are in the fingertips
I use to trace your words. I put your memory of plants,
animals, and us in things I can hold. They are small.
I have tried to carve them in stone and wood. My failures
come not from a lack of skill. They come from the
struggle I have of missing you.

He learned to spin. The two holy men who taught him to spin called it whirling. They disagreed on what it achieved. One saw it as means to keep the devil from their lives. One saw it as a means to get closer to the Holy One.

AN ACOLYTE CROSSES THE PLAZA. She locks her hands behind her back. She sees a horse without rider gallop past her. Thinking it is a sign that her life is a lie, she pulls her hands apart. She throws herself to the ground. She cries out that she should be dead.

A boy skips across the plaza. His right foot touches every third brick. At the end of the plaza, he squats. He counts the bricks he has touched on his fingers. A passer-by looks at him and shakes her head.

A street-cleaner sweeps the plaza, starting at its east end. He carries a sack to throw paper and other trash in. He sings a slow tempo ballad. A shop owner passes him. He bends down and picks up the paper he drops. He stops the cleaner and drops the paper in the sack.

Pigeons circle above the cleaner. They fly down to the part he has cleaned. New pigeons fly down to each new part he cleans. The plaza fills up with pigeons when he is done. The cleaner pulls out some seeds from a small bag. He walks among the pigeons and throws the seeds around him. The pigeons feed on the seeds. The cleaner walks to a new part of the plaza. He throws more seeds in the air. The pigeons do not fight among themselves. The street-cleaner places his sack on the ground. He spreads his arms out. He spins around until the pigeons eat the seeds he leaves for them. He picks up his sack and leaves the plaza.

It is said that truth is allusive. This
may come from what lies underneath truth.
A lie may stay hidden under a truth.

THERE ARE NO TRUTHS I HAVE not destroyed. You do not see them. You define what is good. Yet, what you do goes against it. You believe in the power of mercy. Yet, you hold it back when it is most needed. You speak of justice. You hold it up as if it were a sun that sheds light everywhere. Yet you lie. You pervert your courts. Your last act shows the power of what I can do. You hold your hands to your heart. You ask your Gods to forgive you. Yet, you continue to do what you asked forgiveness of. You continue to do what you know is unjust. You continue to lack mercy. This last act shows I have succeeded more than I thought I could.

The weight of a truth or a lie is not
counted in pluses and minuses. They have
their own means of counting.

WE HAD THEM LINE UP ALONG the wall. The adults
were behind the children. We asked that their leader
come out from among them. A girl of nine or ten
stepped forward. We shouted, *You lie to us. One more
lie, and we will shoot all of you.* A boy stepped forward.
He looked to be the same age as the girl. It was
useless. A second threat would have another child
step forward. We left them. They were better liars
than we were. We had come for information.
The dead would not tell us what we wanted to know.

I have a name. I have no name. It is
how I keep my power. One I know. The other
is what others wish they could call me.

I AM YOUR FRIEND IN THIS GAME. If you think
I will stay your friend, you are fools. I am one of the
deceivers. We come. We take on the form you want.
We return to being who we are when you are at your
most vulnerable. That is when we can do the most harm.
It may be a small lie that leads you to believe others.
We prefer these. They are more dangerous than the
big lies. They are like a worm. They become part
of you. You start to lie when you don't need to. You become
a reflection of who we are. You are our small mirrors.
A truth or a better lie can shatter you. This is our goal.
You destroy who you are. We don't have to see it.
The shards of this act are all we need to see.

I have a name. I have no name. It is
how I keep my power. One I know. The other
is what others wish they could call me.

I AM A SAVAGE. I fight with whoever comes
before me. The only virtue I have is I do not hold
back. I kill all those I fight. My name is a secret.
I keep it from those I kill and from those I generously
let go. I know there is a conflict in what I say.
There are more of me. My race is just like me.
They are hidden. They give my fearsome acts more
power. I am compared to being a God. It is all in
my favor. I am not like a God who can be just and
merciful. I am the taker of life. My kind follows
my lead. We watch you. You have become like us.
We know this will be our end. It is a terrible choice.
Exist with limited power. End who we are.

The game of chess and killing have
some things in common. Taking pawns leads
to taking Queens and Kings. Lying can lead
to killing. The two acts are not the same. The
end could be same.

I WATCHED THOSE WHO WALK across the
pedestrian bridge above the subway tracks. I started
this practice with my first lie. It was not the small
lie that we tell others. I lie. Someone dies. I took the
identity of my second kill. He lived in a small town in
the Southwest. I killed him with my own hands. I kill.
It is like the game of chess, taking a pawn is only the
first move. The Queen and the King are the big moves.
Taking a life is the big move. I do it by lies that can't
be traced to me.

The soul is lost when its light is not partnered with the darkness in the one who creates us all.

I STRUGGLE TO UNDERSTAND your truths. Others say I am a fool. We shouldn't question you. I look at my hands before I bring them to my face and cover my eyes. It is all I have to calm the conflict that takes place within my soul. I don't speak of it to others. It is terrifying enough to feel it. My soul reflects the conflict in you. I know this because my soul is only a shard of your power.

Some rules come from what we
observe. Others are simply what we should do.

LLOYD FOUND THAT HE COULD set out the
rules of behavior in four observations. He wrote them
in a journal and never put anything in it after that.

Observe

An act made in a calm state is a true act.

Observe

Words and hurtful behavior can have
the same result.

Observe

Courtesy and politeness are not the
same. Politeness has a dark side. It can
be used to show or believe one is more
cultured or refined than others. Courtesy
is the simple act of being respectful and
considerate of others.

Observe

What is said or is done can come from
conscious or unconscious causes.

I read her prayer-like words. I saw my father and her dance. I knew I would find my own joy.

FATHER AND MOTHER DANCE before the earth that holds them. They circle around me. Mother leans in. She tells me they are happy. It is time for me to find my own happiness. Father takes my hand. He says to dance with them for the last time. I read the journal she left me. It was mother's way of saying she knows I will go on. She never told me of her dream. I reread the lines of her inked calligraphy. I knew I would find something from my father. It would be something I could wear to remind me of the joy they had.

An ear-wick and a confession have a
thing in common. They don't get lost on
their own.

I CAN'T FORGET THE SCENE. The body of the
one I killed lay on the ground. I heard Dion singing
"Higher than Heaven" from the CD in his car. I had
pulled him from the car. I put a Saint Christopher
medal in his right hand. I put a mezuzah and Islamic
prayer beads in his left. It became my calling card.
I was known as the three-religion killer. Each time
I killed, I left my card. I could hear Dion singing of
being higher than heaven when he went out with
his girl. It was just how I felt with my killings.

When you come to do something hard
to do, you want more. That thing may not come.

HE WATCHED A PEASANT WALK beside a
hoofed animal. A boy was with the peasant. He watched
as the peasant looked over the side of the trail. He watched
some rocks come loose. They fell into the river below.
He heard the sound of the rocks echo off the mountain.
He saw the peasant and the boy build a crude plank
bridge for the animal to cross. He heard the animal
bay as it was urged to cross the bridge.
 He was a watcher. He saw scenes and remembered
them. He felt strange. He had become what he had wanted.
He wanted more. He was more than a watcher. He watched
what others did. He wanted to know if others watched
him with such dispassion. He had one thing left to do.
He would watch himself. He knew that it would be
hard.
 He watched the peasant, boy, and animal move
up toward the snowline until he could not see them.
He walked back to the valley. He walked to the hut he
lived in. He knew what he would do. He would record
it all in a journal. He knew it would take time. Hope
and doubt would not be easy to give up. They would
die off. He knew he would watch. He knew he would hear.
He knew it would become enough.

I confess. I want revolution. I want
fast change.

I HOLD NO FASCINATION WITH the torture of
animals and people. I allow one exception to such torture.
If it leads to the annihilation of groups of animals and
people, it is justified. Torture in the singular is a waste.
It will not be a success. It will not bring change.
It will not bring a new order. I do not mean evolution.
I mean a quick change. Actions and languages will not be
separate. The idea of oneness will be consumed by this
species. It will practice it. It will not kill to eat or to
win lands or followers. This species will be unique.
Its growth will not be evolution. It will be revolution.
One idea will be its guide. Its leaders will give it a
simple name. They will call it PEACE.

24.8, 25.8, 29.5. They are numbers.
They could be more. It is for the wise
to decide.

THE HEBREWS WERE A WISE people. They hid
in the *Aggadah* a part of the *Halachah* that said the
holy writings could be saved from fire on the Sabbath.
Hidden in legend was law. A God and its people are
wise when they both make exceptions to preserve
their holy words. This wisdom appeared again in
their writings. At times, it was left out. Disputes arose.
In rare cases, it led to killings. It was not from the dispute.
It came from those who did not accept that a God
could be argued with. That a God could change
its mind.

Soldiers can carry guns and knives.
They can carry other things. These can be
more dangerous than weapons can be.

THE SOLDIERS DID NOT CARRY guns or knives.
They came with their own weapons. They had harmonics.
As soon as they began to play them, cracks in the
earth appeared. The rocks and vegetation flew into
the air. When the soldiers stopped playing, cracks
appeared in all the homes in the village. Pieces from
them flew into the air.

The leader of soldiers grew. When he was eleven
feet tall, he spoke to the people who had run from
their homes. Where they stood, the earth was solid.
The leader of the soldiers raised his arms. He spread
them out then brought them back to his sides. The pieces
of the homes returned to where they had been.
The rocks and what vegetation the earth once held
returned to where they had been.

The leader said that they would return if the
villagers did not stop their bad ways. He said that
they had to stop lying, stealing, and killing. If they
did not, they would return. They would not play their
harmonics. They would sing and all living things
would die .

He said that his men and he could not bring life
back. His men and he turned their backs on the villagers.
They marched off. As they reached the outskirts of the
village, they flew into the air.

The villagers broke into two groups. The ones

who stayed followed what the soldiers told them to do. The ones who wanted to keep their old ways left the village. As they reached its outskirts, a flute was heard. The bad villagers could not move. They started to lose pieces of their bodies. They flew into the air. They were not seen again.

The sins of fathers can be passed to
their sons. It can make the sons get revenge for
what their fathers did to those close to them.

WHEN HE LEFT HER FOR A younger woman,
his wife fled to the mountains. The townspeople never
heard from her again. Ten years later, their son came back.
He was a grown man. He carried a gun. When he
found his father, he held him up. He tied his father up.
He took out a small branding iron with the words **NO
GOOD** on it. Then he built a fire and put the iron in it.
When the iron was red hot, he branded his father in
four places. The words **NO GOOD** were burned into his
palms and the backs of his hands. The townspeople
didn't blame him. The father had abandoned his sister
and him when he took up with the other woman.
The son left. He became a legend. Children would call him
the good one. Adults would treat each other better.
They were afraid the ones they might hurt would do a
similar thing to them.

If you see a woman doctor with a
holster on her hip, she could heal you. She
could pull her pistol and shoot you if you
wrong others. She has two ways to bring
peace. One is to heal you. The other is to
warn you to stop your bad ways.

SHE CAME TO TOWN. Her face and her hands
showed the signs of abuse. An old couple took her in.
They had lost their two boys to wars. They never asked
her how she got the wounds and the scars they left.
She became a nurse. The couple were both doctors.
They taught her everything they knew. They also taught
her how to use a gun. She healed the sick. She protected
those who were threatened. She never married. She took
in two orphans. Like the old couple, she taught them
what she knew. It was no surprise. They became healers.
They came to protect those who were threatened.

Others had lived in caves. They were not hermits. They were not diseased. They needed the aloneness. It gave them a place to practice their faith.

THEY LIVED IN A CAVE. People said that they had committed a horrible crime. They had a reason. They could not practice their faith with such people. They believed that the Holy One could be a bear, a falcon, or a fish. It could be an insect. If it tried to be a human, it would burn up and die. Such a simple belief was dangerous. It could lead to their death. It could lead to others taking up their belief. Then they would not be alone to speak to the Holy One. This would be harder than living in a cave.

Revenge is done to right a wrong. It is done so one can be at peace. There are other reasons for doing it. They do not matter. It is for the one who takes revenge to decide if it is right or wrong.

IF YOU SEE HIM, DON'T TELL ME. I will look for him. I know what will happen. I will shoot him. Then I will use the gun to kill myself. What he did to my children left me with one reason to live. It is to kill him. I need to find him on my own. My revenge will be complete. Life without my children is hard. It is harder knowing he lives. I can join my children after I take his life. People may make a song of what I did. They may say nothing. It doesn't matter. My revenge will be complete.

Sometimes one thing can contain two things in it. Music and words can be happy. They can be happy and sad. They are mirrors of who we are.

COME DANCE WITH ME. The music is happy. The lyrics are sad. They are like our lives. Come dance. Forget the sadness. Forget the words we say to make others feel sad. Come dance. Enjoy the music and the peace and happiness it brings. This is our secret. This is why I ask you to dance with me. The music is happy. It is what counts. The lyrics are sad. Forget the words and the sadness they hold. Come dance with me.

Others have said it in their way. The just life is based on not bringing harm to the ones you come in contact with.

HE KEEPS ONE OF THE HOLY one's pages in a glass frame. This is how he keeps his promise to his mother. It is to live a just life. He doesn't follow her faith. His promise has to do with acting justly. It has to do with not causing harm to others.

ه درمیگ دیوار بشنوه

beh dar migam, divar beshnaveh
I am telling the door so that the wall will hear it.

- Persian Saying

THEY CAME TO ME. They said I could help them. I knew the way. I knew the way through the mountain. I had taken others to safety, but the last group I helped was four years ago. They sold two of their boys into slavery.

I said I would help them. I asked them to wait while I went to get some things I would need from the study. Once there, I opened the desk's bottom drawer. I took out a small statue of a horse with a rider on it. I placed it on the floor. I sat next to it and repeated the words my grandfather taught me. The rider slid off the horse and grew into a replica of me. When it reached my size, we exchanged clothes, and I told him what to take from the closet. Before he left, he stood next me and touched my left ear. As I started to shrink to his original size, he promised he would lead them in circles.

They would get mad at him. They would either abandon him and return to their land or throw him off the mountain. He would fall into the air and shrink down to his original size as he fell out of sight of his killers. He would fly back to me, and we would exchange sizes. The killers would find a map on the ground. It would only show them how to get to their land.

I would return the statue back to his place in the drawer after we both drank a cup of dandelion tea. And we thanked my grandfather for his gift and the words he taught me.

ه در می‌گم دیوار بشنوه
beh dar migam, divar beshnaveh
I am telling the door so that the wall will hear it.
- Persian Saying

MY BIRTH TOWN WAS HARDLY known outside of those who lived there. If others knew of it, it was because the rivers in the area around it had some of the finest white water rafting in the state. When I moved out-of-state, people would ask me where I came from. They would have the same blank stare as my younger brother when he was asked if he had done something wrong. I would say that there were great rafting rivers around it.

After a year of this type of dialogue, I looked into the history of my hometown. That is when I found out that a deranged ex-husband blew up a school bus of children in the 1920's. No one in town spoke about it because of the horrendous outcome. All the children and their driver were killed. Now, I had something I could say to people, but I did not say it. I chose to respect the suffering the incident left. When I asked my mother about it, she told me the same thing that was in the newspapers. She added, "Jesse, my parents never spoke about it with me."

She said that she only found out because her grandfather was the driver, and her mother or father took her to school. "It was like that for all the families in town. We kids were driven by our parents to school."

Words can be read even when they
are not on paper.

MASTER, WE TOOK YOUR BOOKS, your smokes.
We knew you would be mad. We had to do it. You
said we should give up our possessions. You said they
held us back. We did not want to see you shamed. You
would look at your books, your smokes. You would
look at our clothes, our shoes. You would see it was
all we had. We would need to leave you if you held on
to your books, your smokes. Master, it is your choice.
Master, make it.

If God is just and merciful, we must do those things being people of faith.

A FRIEND SENT ME A LETTER with an article that he found online. The article is on the brothers Hamid and Xhemal Veseli of Albania who were honored by *Yad Vashem* (The World Holocaust Remembrance Center) of Israel for saving Jews from the Nazis during the War.

My friend fleshed it out. The Muslims of Albania believe that all persons are from God. It is part of the Muslims hospitality to strangers. The other part is connected to the code of *Besa*. He explained that *Besa* is the highest moral code of Albania. It means *to keep the promise*. If you follow the code, you keep your word. One can trust his or her life and the lives of their family to those who keep *Besa*. Those who save a life enter paradise. *Besa* says that all of us are God's children. They are our children too, and we must treat them as our own.

My friend said that *Besa* is embedded in the *Kanun* – a set of customary laws started in the fifteenth century. In article 601 of the *Kanun*, it is stated, "The house of an Albanian belongs to God and the guest." He said this idea shows the difference between religion and faith. Faith is the practice of living a just and a merciful life, and not just saying words of the religious.

The Veseli brothers said their country's Muslims believed if a person comes to your home, you take him or her in. They are a blessing from God. They come before your family and you.

My friend ended his letter to me with the simple statement that we should keep such a practice. He did not use belief. We had discussed over the years that the pairing of belief and act is not kept by many.

thrown rock
skips across lake's surface
circles touch its sides

HE OPENED THE BOOK TO ITS first page. The author introduced Yosa Buson, the haiku poet, with a reference to him walking in a field where he sees a thorn bush. It is in bloom with small white flowers. It gives off a strange fragrance. The poet stops and writes a haiku alluding to memories of his childhood. In the next paragraph, the author says Buson never returned to his childhood home although he lived thirty miles from it for the rest of his life.

Unlike the haiku poet, he kept moving further from his childhood home. He has described it so well in stories that a friend got around it without asking directions.

As Buson had done, he broke physical ties with the neighborhood where he was raised. He was twenty-three at the time. At nineteen, he went to school in another state. From fifteen, he lived in rural communes. He returned once to the city he had left, but he didn't go back to his neighborhood. He kept up with its physical changes through magazines, photo collections, and internet searches. As Buson, he may need those memories of his childhood home to blend a place with time and emotion.

Some stories can be told in songs.
Some stories come from songs. Listen to
both. They are good stories.

THEY TELL ME YOU'RE GONE. I listen to the
wind. I listen to the falling leaves. They whisper they
can't say they killed you. I feel the loss in the water I
take to clean the dirt from my hands and face. I feel
like I am in a song. I feel like the bandit who learned
to love while running from the law. He winds up in
Mexico. He can't cross the border. They'll track him
down and kill him. Even worse, they'll catch him.
And she'll see him hang for the crimes he committed.
After they leave, I plan my revenge. I know it may
take a year before they feel safe. Meanwhile, I'll play
the fool. Then I'll kill them all in one day. That day,
I'll visit your grave and confess my crime. I'll then be
ready to die and join you.

The ancients would not talk for eight months before being parents for the first time. They believed that it would help them listen to others. They learned how words could harm others.

"THE WOMAN LOOKS DULL-WITTED." The words look almost innocent on paper. Kurt reads them aloud. He has to hear them. He has to give them a sense of realness. Why would one say it? Kurt could not imagine saying it. It could be true. You keep that to yourself. Gossips say such things. He avoids such people. His mother says, "Teeth and lips guard against what the tongue could do." She means the harm words could do. They could be relentless. They would be when they say what acts harmed people. If he is asked why he does not gossip, he says he has inherited it. He leaves it there.

These confessions, these inner thoughts,
these histories demand that they be heard in
silence. It is true. It is the only way we will
take in what they say.

*I CONFESS. I AM NOT STILL. My soul is not
at peace. It reflects the turmoil we create. My soul
should be still. Be the home, be the resting place,
of peace. It cannot be as long as I lie, steal, and kill.
You cannot be still.* When I read your words, the joy I
thought I would have is not there. They turn against
themselves. They call out they have been deceived.
The answer lies in a dream. Yet I am afraid. What if it
is there and not there? I will wake more lost. I must
ask if it will show me what to do. This is my last hope.

Blessed are those who keep their faith.
It doesn't matter if it has nothing to do with
religion or the rituals of them.

WE COVER HER HANDS WITH a cloth. She looks down at her hands. She tells us her name. We know it. We wait for her to start her story. It is the same. She starts by telling us where it takes place. She follows this by when. The stories are amazing. Each is a world of its own. We can't tell you them. They are her confessions. She is not religious, but she treats them like prayers. They are to be shared by her and those she confesses them to.

There are times you can't say why
friends are friends. They just are.

I HAVE MY HARDEST FIGHTS with you. Your questions frighten me. You ask me to prove something. You ask me to argue against something. You ask that I speak, hearing my silence.

I say no, yet you still ask that I speak. After our fights, I realize you knew what I would say.

There is little to do when you are told
to do nothing. The meaning is to do nothing to
call attention to you. A sage, a man of wisdom
does not speak these words. They are spoken
by those who couldn't do it.

YOU WERE TOLD TO BE GOOD. Those words
had a meaning you understood. They contained the
threat of being punished. It wasn't physical. You could
be deprived of some thing. With your children, you
are careful. You explain what is expected of them.
That something they do troubles you. It is not who
they are. The implication of hurt in good is too strong
to repeat it with your children. It is enough that they
see you act fairly with others and with them. They
will know you mean what they are doing and not who
they are.

The line that cuts history and myth changes. It changes when animals are in the making of myth.

THE MASTER SAT BY THE POOL. He kept his legs in a full lotus. He picked up a small stick by his right foot. He used it to write the same word on top of itself in the earth by his left foot. *Wait.* While writing the word, he repeated the mantra "In Out Nine Doors" he chose when he first learned to sit. When the nuns found him in the morning, he still had the stick in his hand. The nuns did not touch him. Three mice stood by his right foot. You could see their breath in the cool air. The Master's skin had begun to turn a reddish gray color. He did not have the odor of death. The nuns left him. They returned for the next three days. Each time, they saw more of the Master's skin deepen its color. Then they would leave. Each day one less mouse stood by his right foot. On the fourth day, the head of the order joined the other nuns. She bent down and touched the hand that held the stick. It had turned to stone. The Master and the stick he held had turned to stone.

The page and what is not seen on it are
like the finch and the falcon. One invites you.
One keeps you from it. The one like the finch
quickens the air. You recognize it as the amazing.
The one like the falcon moves at another level.
You come to see it as a warning.

WHEN I HEARD THAT VOICE read your words,
I slowed my breath. I wanted the words to fall into
my body as the quickened air that finches make
as they hover about a feeder. I would be the seeds
they fed on. Then I heard the words not on paper.
They disturbed me. At first, it was a small itch.
I could put up with it. Then it took another form.
It seemed too proud. I recognized what it was. They always
referred back to you. The beauty of the words on
paper I could have as an intimate friend. The boasting,
self-promoting, words not on paper had the warning
of the end of any friendship I could have with you.

Some rituals can't be explained.
They are done. If there is pleasure in them,
it is just part of doing what brings joy.

SHE SAT BY THE STREAM. She dipped a hand
in it. She took it out. She watched the water slide off
the hand. She took out a slice of bread she had
carried in her bag. She broke it into small pieces,
threw them on the stream's surface. She turned
and walked away. She didn't need to see fish
nibble at them.

I saw some people starving
There was murder, there was rape
Their villages were burning
They were trying to escape.
    – *Almost the Blues*, Leonard Cohen

I WALKED WITH MY UNCLE on the dirt road to his home at the top of the hill. He could sit on its deck and see our valley. When we stood on the deck, he asked me to sit with him on one its benches. He called me son. He spoke to me in his rough voice. I knew I should be quiet. It was his way to say I should listen to what he said.

He started to sing the first five lines of Leonard Cohen's song "Almost the Blues." Joe knew the words and music to Cohen's songs. He had all his albums. He had played tapes for me of Cohen's live performances he got from a friend whose father was in Cohen's band. My uncle smiled. "I know you want to know why I use Cohen's lines before I read Joseph's letter. You'll see." He called his son Joseph.

Joe's letter matched the darkness of the opening of Cohen's song. He spoke of dead bodies on streets. Boys and girls whose starving bodies couldn't protect their bones. Houses in rubble, on fire. He spoke of how he had to shoot one of his men. He saw the man raping a village girl. He shot him in the leg. He pulled him off the girl. He cleaned the wound and bandaged it. The other men didn't report him. Joe had saved their lives more than once. The rapist knew he would have to answer to the men if said what Joe did.

When my uncle finished Joe's letter, he handed it to me. His hands shook freely. He looked at me. The tears in both our eyes showed the love we had for Joe and for the pain his letter expressed.

Clothing can come with a history.
They can bring up the joy and the sadness
of those who wore them.

I PUT ON DAD'S FLAT BRIM, Amish hat he first wore in college. I wanted to see how I would look in it. He had steamed it, so the brim bent slightly down in the front. I looked in the mirror. I knew Mom would cry if she saw me in it. The first time they were together he was wearing it. She gave Dad a lift to campus in her beat up Yugo. It was one of her best stories about him. He thanked her and sat silently after he answered where he needed to go. She would say a man in an Amish hat, lamb's wool coat, and real leather mailbag was a dish. She had seen him walking to campus many times before, so she was surprised he was hitching. She wanted to ask why, but he sat in a stilled silence. He looked as if he were meditating. When she dropped him off at the green houses, she asked for his number. Dad looked surprised. He asked her for her number. He said he would call her. They saw each other for two years before they got married. They finished their degrees. Dad went with her to Boston where she had her psych residency. He wore the hat until he had cancer and died.

HE GOT DIZZY READING IN the car. It worried him.
It had happened when he got up too quickly from
sitting or lying down. While speaking to a friend
about it, he learned that reflected light of the sun
could cause him to feel dizzy. He said he would
try it when it was gray. "I mean a fully gray sky.
It's the scientific way." They both laughed at his way
of saying compare and judge.

Some letters are gifts and reminders.
They are kept for what they say or show.

A FRIEND MAILED ME A PAGE from *The New York Review of Books.* It had an etching of Samuel Beckett. He said I should keep it. Beckett was one of us. Yet his eyes keep him from us. They saw all. Like a heavenly Lord, the picture of Beckett would remind me that there are those among us who can see to the deepest part of our soul.

My story is in the words that others
speak. I cannot talk. I can only write words.

I WALK IN WORN SANDALS. I wear a coat with patches, a pair of slacks rescued from the trash of others. My shirt and socks are my own. They are in good shape. I have three new items. They are two notepads and a pen. I use them to write. I can't talk. I am one of the lucky ones. People know me. I am called Notepad Man. Children love to read my notes. I draw pictures for some of the words. Parents and adults buy large pads for me, so I can draw pictures for the children. I leave the pictures with them. This gift of mine brings me the gift of food and shelter. There are times when the children walk with me. They go to see friends in the next village. They are my protectors. When I leave them, I promise to see them again. This is easy for me. I have no set place I have to be.

Some say that hurt and pain are the same thing. You can hurt something. It's simple. Hurt can cause pain. Pain can't cause hurt. Even this is too simple. Hurt and pain can be the same at times.

I KNOW I HURT YOU. I know you still hurt. I wish I could take that hurt and wash it away. Away as easily as I wash my hands and face in the morning before I ask forgiveness for what I do. I know these are only words. Each day, I try to be caring and kind. I know it can't take the pain you feel. It helps me live with the pain I found I caused. I know I will still hurt, even if you forget your hurt. I could live with that. Maybe, I will cry for you, the pain I brought to you. I know the pain I have will stay with me. If it is not in what I say, it will be in my dreams.

They call it the water blues. It's really
the crashing waves and smell of salt in the air.

I WAS IN MEMPHIS SEEING a friend and her man.
She didn't call him her lover or her friend. We went
to hear some music. I took some time on my own
to explore the city. I took a two-day trip to Oxford,
Mississippi. I wanted to see Faulkner's home. I left
two days after coming back. We had planned for me
to stay a week more. I was anxious to be home. I told
my friend I had to leave. I had to be by the ocean.
I had been by the great body of water so long I felt
lost being away from it. I had to hear crashing waves,
smell salt in the air. That without them, I felt I was
not alive.

Some things show they are rich.
Some things symbolize what they love.

THERE WERE BOXES OF BOOKS and albums on
the floors. Jim had helped Sue box them. They belonged to
her sister. They were two of the three kinds of things
she would keep. She also had all the letters her sister
had sent her. They were divided into two parts.
The first part spoke of what she had done. The second
part spoke of the books that she read or the songs
she listened to. Marie had been a librarian. It seemed
natural she would have over six thousand books.
The number of albums surprised Jim. He had counted
all of them. There were three thousand and ten.
Sue laughed when he told her the number. "Jim, music
and writing have rhythms and patterns. Lyrics are
just another form of writing." He smiled. June was a
nurse. Her sister cared for what people made.
She cared for people.
 Sue had stethoscopes. The count was twenty.
Three of them were nearly a hundred years old.
The sisters collected things that symbolized what
they did. He knew June would give him the books and
albums to keep at his place. She had done it with four
of her stethoscopes. They would be married in two
months. He knew their new home would need a room
for the books and albums. He had built a cabinet to
hold the stethoscopes. It had glass doors and shelves.
He would start on bookcases. He would read up on
what he could make to hold the albums.

The earth and the sounds that surround us are part of who we are. A wise person never forgets that.

"THERE IS NOTHING LIKE LYING on the earth. Yes, and listening to the sounds around you." Those two sentences were spoken by her best friend before she got up and walked off. Marie would not see her again. She could say those sentences when she wanted. She had repeated them as her friend walked off. She knew them as if they were own words. She knew her friend had given her a way to live. That night she wrote in her journal. She put two straight lines under the sentences. They were to remind her of her friend and wish her good luck. When she would think of earth, she would think of Joan. When she would think of Joan, she would think of earth.

There are ways to get information.
You get more if you stay with the line of
identifying and showing respect. It is not
in your manual. It's what you learn in the field.

"WE HEARD HE DIED. We are looking for someone who knew him." The detective kept what he said simple to match the old man's way of saying things. He kept what he said grammatically correct. He didn't want the old man to feel he had made fun of him. When he found out what he needed to know he thanked the old man. "Sir, we thank you for what you told us. Here's my card. Call me if you want to speak to me or remember something you think we should know."

The prayer for the dead starts with praising God. The more intimate one may start with the names for the dead or who they were.

"THIS IS IT." He pointed to the building where he grew up. "This is where they hid me. They were my parents' servants. They became my family, and this place, my home. They raised me as if I were theirs." His hand trembled as he touched the mailbox where their name had been. His daughter rang the bell for 4-B. He softly started the prayer for the dead as they walked up to the fourth floor. He stopped at the second floor. "It's okay! I have finished my prayer. Dear children give me a few minutes to tell you what happened. This is where my life began. My birth parents fled without me. I never saw them again. After the war, they didn't return. Father John and Mother Helga had seen them. They heard that they no longer wanted me." When they reached the fourth floor, he asked his son to knock on the door. As they waited for an answer, he took the hands of the two children by his sides. He silently offered his own prayer. *Mother, Father, may I live to be the son you raised me to be.* The three of them stood there. A father, a son, a daughter waited for the door to open.

I wish there was a song for talk, talk, talk; try a little silence. There is a song "Try a Little Tenderness." Maybe that's where I got my idea.

I WOULD NOT SPEAK. You tried to break my silence. You couldn't. I had stopped talking to save what I had worked hard to learn. All around me people talked. It was noise. I heard content. Some talk had facts I could find in print. Some talk had opinions. I heard them on the radio. Almost none of the talk had substance and passion. I needed both of them to stay alive. I chose not to talk to protect them. When I heard talk with them, I would give a note to the people who had them. I kept this tentative contact with others. I knew without them I would die. I would take my own life.

They say water is precious. It is a
limited resource. They are not wrong. Yet we
have a more intimate answer. We used it to
wash our hands and face before we pray.

IN OUR CITY, WATER WAS LIKE GOLD. It was
not precious because we had so little of it. We used it
to clean ourselves. We drank it without worrying how
much we had. We cooked with it. We nourished our
plantings with it. What made it precious was that we
used it to wash our hands and face before we prayed.

When it came to say who they were,
they would say they were The People. It may
be that they led a simple life. It may be they
simply thought that was who they were.

WE WHO LIVED ON THE SHORT side of the
mountain had a word for those on the other side.
We called them The West People. We did not call
ourselves the East People. We were simply The People.
The sea was never more than a few miles from the
mountain. A few of us lived on the mountain. Even less
of us lived in one of its valleys. The rest of us lived on
the land between the sea and the mountain. We had a
hard life. Our children were a gift. We said that because
many of them would go off to the sea when they were adults.
They would look for other places to live. Those who
would come back would not say why. They would
burn our bodies when we died. They would place the
ashes in two pouches. They would take one pouch to
the sea and let its ashes fall on to it. They would take
one pouch to the mountain and let its ashes fall on to it.
We no longer knew how it started. It was similar to
our name. It was simply what we did.

People tell us things. When they take other's words and add to them, these words may be guidelines for us.

MY AUNT WAS THE WISE ONE in our family. We were waiting for the elevator one day when she took my hand. "Let's go. I need to speak to you." When we were in the courtyard of our building, she handed me a paper written in calligraphy. She usually gave me notes in a script form. These were in a print form.

"1. *Live calmly*, performing your *daily duty*.
2. Always keep your heart pure, and act according to its dictates.
3. Respect your ancestors.
4. Make the *Mikado's will yours and carry it out*.

"These are the four great imperatives that govern the Japanese soul. The Japanese do not care about the awesome problems of metaphysics. Unlike the Hindus, they are not willing to lose their personality and vanish in the universe. Where the world comes from, where it is going—these are not questions that concern them. Wide intellectual horizons strike them as dim and sterile. They narrow their glance to take in the limited fullness of earth and sea, of the mounds of bones and ashes of their ancestors, of the threshing-floor of their country.

For the Japanese, the supreme, the only creative duty
of man is to work and function within the narrow
circle of his race."
          She explained that Mikado meant Emperor.
She said that the third and the fourth imperatives
were unique to Japan. We had to respect all people.
It did not mean we should be blind to their faults.
She paused. She said that it means to be courteous.
I should think of it that way. I knew what she meant.
She was careful with how she treated others. She stayed
calm even if she was not pleased with what others did.
She explained the fourth imperative by saying to
replace the Emperor with a mentor. We should listen
and watch him or her. See what they do. Listen to
what they say. They are able to show us how to live.
She smiled and warmed me to be careful whom I
would choose. Such people were not emperors.
They were humans. They had good and bad sides.
They could show us how to act. She looked down at
her hands. She said that they could show us how not
to act. I wanted to ask her who had written what was
on the note. She said she knew what I wanted to ask.
The Greek writer and poet Nikos Kazantzakis had put
them in his chapter on the city of Kobe, in his book
Japan China. She said that Dad had a copy. He also had
his other books that were translated into English.

In the past, a great thinker said a
citizen could take a ruler's life. He or she
would need a good reason. This was not all.
They would lose their own life.

OUR LORD GREW SOFT. He wore rings on all
his fingers. He wore rows of bracelets on his wrists
and his ankles. We heard talk that he had lost
his power. He was no longer a warrior. He could not
protect us. We stopped bringing tributes to him.
We started to protect ourselves. We had to do the one
thing left to do. We killed him. It was what showed us
how powerless he was.

The dead have stories. The ones who know them may not be the ones we expect to know them. They may not be family or friends. They may be the ones who care for them when no one else would.

WE FOUND HER LYING ON the ground. Her hair was matted. The fingers on her left hand looked as if they had been broken many times. We took off our jackets and covered her. We waited for the ambulance and police to come. They knew who she was. They called her Magic Sally. They said she didn't speak. They said she let her hands speak for her. One of the paramedics said he got so used to her signs, he was able to find out what she wanted. When we asked why she was dead, he made a fist with one hand. He put the other over it. He pulled them apart. He said she had seen too many bad things happen and couldn't handle it anymore. We never forgot his answer. When we go to visit her grave the medic had paid for, we put two small stones on her headstone. Then we pray for both of them.

Some letters are gifts and reminders.
They are kept for what the say or show.

SHE DREW A CRANE AND A POOL to represent rain.
She put the straight line of the bird's wings under a
circle of the pool to mean rain. If she put a zigzag
line in the circle, it meant lightning. The last step
was to put an open triangle touching the circle to
mean wind or thunder. The tip or pointed part of the
triangle was closed. The base was open. She knew
this was the start of their writing. She would take
parts of her curved and straight lines to make the
letters. They would match the sounds of the parts of
their words. Her daughter completed her work. She
had forty letters. Some were one line. Some were two
lines. The last group of letters had three or four lines
in them.

The law has two main forms. The first
is the oral law. It can be forgotten or be easily
changed. The second is the written law. It is
not as easy to forget or to change. It works the
best when people know how to read and write.

THE LEADER SPOKE TO THEM in a voice that
was not his. It said, "There is a time to serve him by
breaking the law." He was their first leader to start
the task of putting the oral laws in writing. The voice
said that all the people would learn to read and write.
They would be able to write on the justice of their laws.
He had the scholars in the land become their teachers.
He had the judges who could read join them.
They taught the people to read and write. These acts
brought peace to the land. Acts of violence, falsehoods,
and mistrust could be put on paper. They would be
a record of what was done. All the people could read
the records. No one wanted their name connected
with such acts.

She had read that you couldn't go
home after you leave. In songs and in life
they mix and go against each other. She had
heard the same about art and words.
They can't mix. She knew that you had to go
beyond what others said. Sometimes, they
work well together.

SHE WATCHED HER SON LAY OUT the pieces
of her brother's Erector set on the floor. He took out
his cell phone and shot a picture of them. Slowly, he
laid out the pieces in rows. Each row was one size.
She thought he would take another picture—seeing
that he paused. He didn't. He closed his eyes. When he
opened them, he began to put the pieces together.
Marie had seen her brother do the same thing.
She closed her eyes. When she couldn't hear the
sound of tin against sheet metal, she opened them.
The order of the pieces changed. He left pieces on
the floor. He gave the others a form. What had been
flat was now three-dimensional. The pieces left on
the floor would be picked up and put back in the
cardboard cylinder that had held them.

Our lives came to be rescued by
our children.

WE CAME HERE. We had no choice. Those
who conquered us and killed our king, made some of
us slaves. They sent the rest of us here. This land
was barren. Its winters killed many of us. They brought
ice storms and endless days of snow. Its summers
killed us too. They were so hot that our youngest
children would die of heat exhaustion. We cried out to
our Lord. We had no answer. Our Lord showed us
no mercy. Our children began to sing the mourners words.
They asked our Lord to bring quick death to them.
They didn't want to see their brothers and sisters die
before them. They didn't what to see their parents die
before them. The Lord came to us. It was in the form
of half lion and half ram. It had wings. It flew across
our land. Our parched fields turned green. The heat
of our summers became warm with light breezes.
The ice and snow of winters became a few days.
When those who had conquered us heard that our
land thrived, they came to our border. They tried to
cross it and kill us. Our Lord came back. It was in its
ram and lion form. It had two sets of wings. The first
set of wings let it fly. The second set of wings beat up
a windstorm. It carried those who came to conquer us.
It threw them against mountains, into seas. They died
from their fall. Landslides buried them. The sea had
its creatures bury them under its floor.

Bravery has more than one form.
Those who demonstrate it may not see
it as that.

THEY WERE MARCHED TO THE RIVER. They were
told to strip, to take off any jewelry they wore. They had
to put them in two piles. One would be for their clothes.
One would be for their jewelry. Some refused. They were
divided into three groups. One did not take off their
jewelry. One kept their shoes and socks on. One took
off their shoes and socks. Then they put their shoes back on.
The ones who refused were thrown to the ground.
They were told to get up. They were told to march
into the river. Again, they refused. They would not
get up. The leader of their captors wanted to shoot them.
His men refused. They knocked him to the ground.
They tied him up and threw him in the river.
They told their captives to get dressed. They could leave.
They said they were sorry for seeing them without clothes.

It's this way. Artists create.
Thieves take.

I AM AN ARTIST. I am a thief. I am a petty thief.
I steal small things, things that I can pay for. They are
things from people who know me. They are what
make me an artist. They allow me to imagine those I
stole from when I am not close to them. They hold a
part of the people I steal from. I create images of
them. I know you think I am lying. I am not. The candy
bar I steal I do not eat. The pencil I take from a
counter I do not use. I keep them with me until I can
make images of them. In time I take the things I steal
somewhere else. I leave them there. I am an artist.
I am a thief. I am a trickster. This is my art – copying
but not real copying. When I take and leave what I
steal from my home, I change it. I no longer hold the
memory of those I steal from. My art becomes art.
People buy my pieces. This is how I live. I am an artist.
I am a thief. I am these things.

The Hebrews imagined the Sabbath,
their own creation, was a queen. They gave
that day a name. They called it "Queen
Sabbath."

THE DAY TOOK ON THE FORM OF wondrous beauty.
It became the day of days. It began with the sunset
of the day before it. It ended with sunset of its own day.
Its companions were the other days. They were not
jealous of the day. They would see other rounds of days.
At that moment the day became a partner in the
creation of all that there was. It was for this reason
the day felt itself lucky. It had one thing left to do.
It wanted to share its luck with the other days. It told
them they had names. At that moment, they knew
their names. They each had a separate name. The day
remained the day.

I will know when I am ready.

A HUGE IRON CUP SITS on the ground a-half-a-mile past a desert billboard. It is fifteen feet high and ten feet wide. An ape sits on its cracked rim. The wind is the ape's companion. It asks if it could comfort the ape. It knows the ape is lost. The ape tells the wind that as long as she sees her blood drip from the cup it is the noon hour. There is nothing the wind can do for her.

Stay away from me. I have become
your enemy. I will fight you with my hands
and with my spoken words. It is the only
way to survive. You won't let your children
come near me. I am cursed, spit on me.

I WAS BORN WITH COLORED SKIN. I had
splotches over my body. I was afraid to count them.
They were pink, red, and beige. Some were nearly black.
My mother was a Jew. My Father was a Muslim. They gave
me the Christian name Christopher. On my first day
of school, a father spit on me. Mothers kept their
children from going near me. Teachers would not look
at me when they called out my name. This did not
stop me. I grew stronger. I was like a starving animal.
I devoured books. I was a mother bear. I fought those
who did not see who I was. This is what my skin gave me.
It made me wise. It made me fearless.

Leave some things alone.
They take place. That is all there
is to them.

THE DOG WAITED BY THE DOOR. When we asked how he had trained her, he said, "Nobody remembers anymore." We thought it was a strange answer. We walked away, leaving him alone. We didn't speak of it. We had learned that he meant no harm. It was just his way of saying he wasn't sure.

יִתְגַּדַּל וְיִתְקַדַּשׁ שְׁמֵהּ רַבָּא (אָמֵן)
Yit'ga dal v'yit'kadash sh'mei raba
(Congregation: Amein)
May His great Name grow exalted and sanctified
(Congregation: Amen.)
– "Mourners' Kaddish"

MY HANDS TREMBLED as I started the Kaddish. My father-in-law took my right hand in his. Although I had married into a family of Sephardim and learned Hebrew at one of their synagogues, I recited the Mourners' Kaddish in my parent's Hebrew, as the Ashkenazi would. I said its consonants and vowels as one who came from an East European descent, my father-in-law as one who came from a Spanish descent. Ashkenazim follow the Palestinian rather than Babylonian Jewish traditions. They have different melodies. Those of the Sephardim seemed more natural to me. My father-in-law had a fine singing voice. Even over my louder voice, I could hear his words. He had switched to my parent's Hebrew. It was all there in the first line. *Yis'gawdawl v'yis'kawdawsh sh'mei rawbaw.* The vowel "a" became "aw." The consonant "t" became "s." My hands stopped trembling. He let go of my hand. We finished the Kaddish in nearly one voice.

It has been said the Japanese make gardens with rocks and sand. There are other ways of making a garden.

THE WORKER SITS ON THE GRASS. His book and drink lie inches from his crossed legs. He has a sandwich in one of his hands. He looks out at the lake. Its surface is nearly flat. There is no breeze. A girl skips a rock across it. Ripples move over the lake. The worker lifts the sandwich halfway to his mouth. He does not bite into it. He uses his other hand to take pieces from it and to throw them on the grass. He watches as pigeons come down and feed on them. The girl and the worker create their own gardens. They are alike. They are simple. They will not last. They come from the mind and the body. They are the same. They are two gardeners without a garden to tend.

One can find their voice in many ways.
When that comes, it may come through an act
that is voiceless.

I WAS SICK WITH THE SADNESS I carried.
I tried to dance. I tried to sing. They said they would
help. They said they would pull the sadness from me.
It failed. I couldn't dance. I couldn't sing. I took a job
cleaning corpses, so they could be buried. When my
work was done, I would step outside. I would dance.
I would sing. It was simple. I could not find peace
until I could care for others.

They found the dogs. They were cut
open from their throats to their stomachs.
They knew who did it. She had done it before.
They couldn't prove it. They heard her boast
how easy it was.

HE TOOK SIX DAYS TO FIND OUT how she
did it. He knew that she had killed his cat. She had hit
two of his neighbors' dogs with her car five months
earlier. They couldn't prove she had done it to taunt
them. She made sure of that. She rode with pictures
she had taken of the dead dogs. When questioned,
she told the police she did it to remind her what
a terrible accident it had been. She said she was
willing to pay for any burial expenses. The owners
had already cremated the dogs. He took six days to
plan his revenge. It was perfect. No one linked her
disappearance to him. They knew she had a sick
brother upstate. They figured she had gone to see him.
Two months later, the brother filed a missing
person's report. The police found nothing suspicious.
She was simply gone.

If you say too much, it could be
difficult for you to trust others. If you say
too little, it could be difficult for others to
trust you. The middle way is how to avoid
these traps. You must be the way. You cannot
make a false move. The middle way does not
forgive mistakes. It gives you one chance at it.

MY DAUGHTER COULD SIT alone without speaking.
It was enough for her to be around me. It was the
same with her brother. One night my wife found her
asleep on the floor of her brother's room. When she
woke our daughter and took her to her own room,
she asked her what she was doing. She said she just
wanted to be close to him. My wife sat by the side of
the bed until our daughter fell asleep. When my wife
told me what happened, we hugged each other. There
was nothing to say. We knew if we had grandchildren,
they would be like her.

We may hear some one say something
that can ruin what we had known about him or
her. This can be the worse moment in our lives.
It can be worse than learning of a weakness we have.

ART CARRIED A BUSINESS CARD encased in
plastic. The card had two lines from the pilot for the
series *Justified*. Art had twenty-five of them made up.
He kept them. He didn't give them out. He carried
one with him. Before he spoke with people he had
to make a point with, he looked at the card. He did
it though he knew the two lines. It was like taking
two breaths or counting one thousand, two thousand
before speaking. A good friend told him he didn't need
the card. He knew the lines by heart. "You do it to get
extra seconds before speaking." Art looked at him.
"It's a good move. I'll think I'll keep it. It's like what
Raylan says to Boyd, 'You make me pull, I'll put you
down.'" He didn't have say that Boyd asked if Raylan
would shoot if he had the chance.

Confession is not always the answer.
It has an appeal. It can give us insights to our
own histories. It can free us. It can leave us
empty. It is not an easy choice.

I GUESS I SHOULD CONFESS. I should tell
them what I had done. It would be like giving them an
insight to why I do things. Then I would feel like I
had to tell them my history. They say I will feel better.
I know they are wrong. I would feel like I had nothing
of my own. I know we are both wrong. There is no
easy ground left to me. Confessing and holding back
play at one another.

In laying out these confessions, scenes, inner thoughts, and histories on paper, I had two goals. The first goal was to show the struggle people have between what is said and what is not said. The second goal was to show the forms of confessions, and if they reveal what is hidden or ask for forgiveness. Or, as in the epigraph to this book, they may do neither of those.

-- *I Kyūu*

colophon
Confessions, by I Kyūu,
was set with SITKA, ABOLITION and HIGHTOWER fonts
by SpiNDec, Port Saint Lucie, Florida
The jacket and covers were designed by
Kris Haggblom, Port Saint Lucie, Florida